Hunting

This edition published 2025
by Living Book Press
Copyright @ Living Book Press, 2025

ISBN: 978-1-76153-921-3 (hardcover)
          978-1-76153-838-4 (softcover)

First published in 1932.

This edition is based on the 1933 printing by The MacMillan Company.

A catalogue record for this book is available from the National Library of Australia

Hunting

by

Edith Patch & Harrison Howe

Contents

3. Hunting in the Park

PART ONE
Hunting for Holes

TED'S HOLE

Ted dug a hole.

He dug the hole with a spade.

Ann came to see Ted's hole.

"Ann, see my hole," said Ted.

Ann said, "It is a big hole."

A GOOD GAME

Uncle Jim came to see Ted's hole.

He said, "It is a big hole.

To-day I saw some little holes."

Ted said, "We will hunt and find the little holes."

Ann said, "It will be a good game."

THE ANT HOLE

Ann found a hole.

It was a little hole.

Some ants dug the hole.

Some ants ran into the hole.

Some ants ran out of the hole.

Each ant had six legs.

Each ant had two feelers
  on its head.

Each ant waved its feelers.

THE MOLE HOLE

Ted found a hole.

It was a little hole.

Moles dug it with their hands.

The moles were blind.

They could dig without seeing.

The blind moles had fur.

Their fur was soft and warm.

Blind Father Mole was a hunter.

Mother Mole was a hunter, too.

They hunted for food.

They hunted in their holes.

They could hunt without seeing.

The moles had a nest.

Their nest was in the hole.

Four baby moles were in the nest.

The four baby moles were blind.

Blind Mother Mole took good care of
    the baby moles.

She could do it without seeing.

THE SWALLOW HOLE

Two birds dug a hole in a bank.

They dug it with their bills.

One bird was Father Bank Swallow.

One bird was Mother Bank Swallow.

They were brown and white.

The birds made a nest in the hole.
Mother Bank Swallow laid four eggs
    in the nest.
She kept the four eggs warm.

A baby bird grew in each egg.
Each bird grew and filled the shell.
The shell broke and the bird hatched.

Father and Mother Bank Swallow
    hunted for flies.
They gave flies to the baby birds in
    the nest.
The baby birds could not hunt for
    their flies.
Father and Mother Bank Swallow
    took good care of them.

One day Ted and Ann found the hole.

They saw Father Bank Swallow hunt.

He took some flies in his bill.

He took them into the hole.

Ted said, "He is a good hunter."

"He is a pretty bird," said Ann.

THE SQUIRREL HOLE

Ted and Ann saw a hole in a tree.

Mother Squirrel ran into the hole.

The squirrel had gray fur and a big
gray tail.

Ted and Ann liked to see her.

Ted put a peanut near the tree.

He and Ann sat on the ground and
they were very quiet.

The squirrel came out of the hole.
She ran down the tree and found the
peanut.

Mother Squirrel made a nest and
  Father Squirrel helped her.
It was in the top of a tree.
It was made with dry leaves.
Four baby squirrels lived in it.
They were not old enough to climb.
Mother Squirrel took care of them.

THE WOODPECKER HOLE

Ted and Ann found a hole in a tree.
The tree was old and had no leaves.

Ted said, "I will climb this tree."

"I will climb it, too," said Ann.

Ted said, "Perhaps a squirrel
    lives in this hole!
    Perhaps a bird lives in it!
    Shall we sit near a bush and watch
    the hole?"

They sat near a bush and were quiet.

Two pretty birds flew to the tree.
One bird was black and white.
She was Mother Woodpecker.
One was black and white and red.
He was Father Woodpecker.
The back of his head was red.
The two birds climbed the tree and
    dug little holes in it.
They found food with their bills.

The woodpeckers had a nest in the
  hole in the old tree.

Five white eggs were in the nest.

Mother Woodpecker laid them there.

She took good care of her eggs.

She sat on them to warm them.

All the eggs needed to be warm.

A baby bird grew in each egg.
It grew too big for its shell.
So it broke the shell and hatched.

All the young birds were hungry.
They could not climb or fly.
Their father and mother fed them.
They ate and grew big and their
    feathers grew, too.
They grew old enough to fly and
    climb and pick for food.

Ted and Ann saw them come out and
    pick little holes in the tree.
They ran to tell Uncle Jim,
    "We saw five young woodpeckers
    with black and white feathers."

THE CRICKET HOLE

A little black cricket had a home in a
hole in the ground.

He had six legs and he could run.

He had wings on his back, but he
could not fly with them.

He made a happy sound with them.

The sound was like, "Cree-cree!"

Ted and Ann found the cricket hole.
They sat on the ground to watch it.
They were quiet while they watched.

Little black Father Cricket came out
    of his hole in the ground.
His two feelers waved and waved.
Two of his wings made no sound.
His two top wings went, "Cree-cree!"

Mother Cricket came to hear him.
Her two feelers waved and waved.
She had six legs and she could run.
She had wings on her back, too.
She could not fly with them or make
    a happy sound with them.
She liked to hear Father Cricket.

Black Mother Cricket made a hole.

She laid her eggs in the hole.

She did not sit on her little eggs.

They were in the ground all winter.

The ground was very cold in winter.

There were baby crickets in the eggs,
but they were too cold to hatch.

But the ground was warm in spring!

So the eggs were warm in spring!

The warm baby crickets hatched.

They all came out of the ground.

They had feelers and waved them.

They had legs and ran with them.

But they had no wings at all.

The young crickets ate and grew.
Wings grew on their backs.
At first, their wings were little.

The crickets ate more and grew more.
At last, they were as big as Father
    and Mother Cricket.
And their wings were as big as the
    wings of old crickets.
Then they were grown crickets.

The sister crickets had quiet wings
    like the wings of Mother Cricket.
But the brother crickets had wings
    like the wings of Father Cricket.
So the brothers made a glad sound.
The sound was like, "Cree-cree!"

THE WOODCHUCK HOLE

Father Woodchuck dug a hole, and
  Mother Woodchuck helped him.
The hole was their home.
There was a nest in the hole.
The nest was made of dry grass.

Baby woodchucks were in the nest.
Mother Woodchuck fed them milk.
The milk was good for them.

They could not run and play while
they were very young.
They could drink milk and grow.

When they were old enough to run,
they played in the sunshine.
The sunshine was good for them.

They could sit on their hind legs.
They could use their paws for hands.

The woodchucks could not say words,
but they could whistle.
That was the way they talked.

One day Ted and Ann hunted and
found the woodchuck hole.

They sat near it and did not talk.
They were quiet while they watched.

Six young woodchucks came out and
played in the sunshine.

Ted and Ann often went to see the
  six young woodchucks play.
They liked to watch them eat flowers
  and leaves.
They liked to hear them whistle.

One day Ann had some candy in her
  hand.
Her hand was on the ground.
One woodchuck found the candy.
He took the candy and held it in his
  little paws and ate it.

Ted and Ann laughed when they saw
  the woodchuck eat the candy.
The woodchucks all ran to the hole
  when Ted and Ann laughed!

THE BUMBLEBEE HOLE

A bumblebee hunted for a hole.

She needed a hole for her home.

The bumblebee hummed with her
wings while she hunted for a home.

The humming was like a song.

At last, the bumblebee found a hole.
The hole was in a mouse nest.
It was an old nest.

The mouse had moved out of it.
The bumblebee liked the old nest,
    and she moved into it.
Then she had a very good home.

The bumblebee made some bee
    bread.
She made it with honey and pollen.

She found nectar in some flowers.
The nectar was like sweet water.
She changed the nectar to honey.

She found pollen in flowers, too.
It was like pretty yellow dust.

Mother Bumblebee laid some eggs.

A baby bumblebee was in each egg.

The baby bees hatched.

They had no legs or wings.

They had no black or yellow hairs.

The baby bees liked the bee bread.

They ate it and grew fat.

The fat baby bees went to sleep.
They rested in their cocoons.

Each bumblebee waked and came out
  of her cocoon.
She was not a baby bee then.
She had six legs and four wings.
She had black and yellow hairs.
She was a grown bumblebee
when she came out of her cocoon.

The grown bumblebees flew to flowers for pollen and sweet nectar.
They hummed with their wings when
  they flew to the flowers.
The humming was like a song.

Ted and Ann saw the bumblebee hole.

The bumblebees saw Ted and Ann.

Their buzzing was a cross sound.

Ted and Ann ran to tell Uncle Jim,
 "The bees were cross and buzzed!"

He said, "They will sting you if you go
 too near their hole.
They take care of their home."

Uncle Jim said, "You may watch bees
when they are in flowers."

So Ted and Ann went to a rose bush.
They were very quiet, and the bumblebees did not sting them.

The bees took pollen from the rose
and hummed with their wings.
The humming was like a happy song.

WHERE AND HOW?

How did Ted dig his hole?

Where were the feelers of the ants?

How did the moles dig their hole?
Where did the baby moles live?

Where do bank swallows dig holes?
How do they dig their holes?
Where do the baby swallows live?
How do swallows find food?

Where was the squirrel hole
Ted and Ann found?
Where did the squirrels
put their dry leaves?

WORD GAME

Where will you put each word?

climb   whistle   food   wings

ground   hole   peanut   milk

Ted and Ann could __.

Ted gave the squirrel a __.

The woodpecker nest was in a __.

Father Cricket made a happy sound
with two of his __.

The cricket eggs were in the __.

The two old swallows gave flies to
their young for __.

The baby woodchucks drank __.

The woodchucks could __.

IF I FIND A HOLE

If I find a hole
  Down in the ground,
I'll keep still
  And not make a sound!

I'll watch for moles
  And woodchucks, too.
If you find a hole,
  What will you do?

If you find a hole
  Up in a tree,
Will you keep still
  As you can be?

PART TWO

Hunting in the School Garden

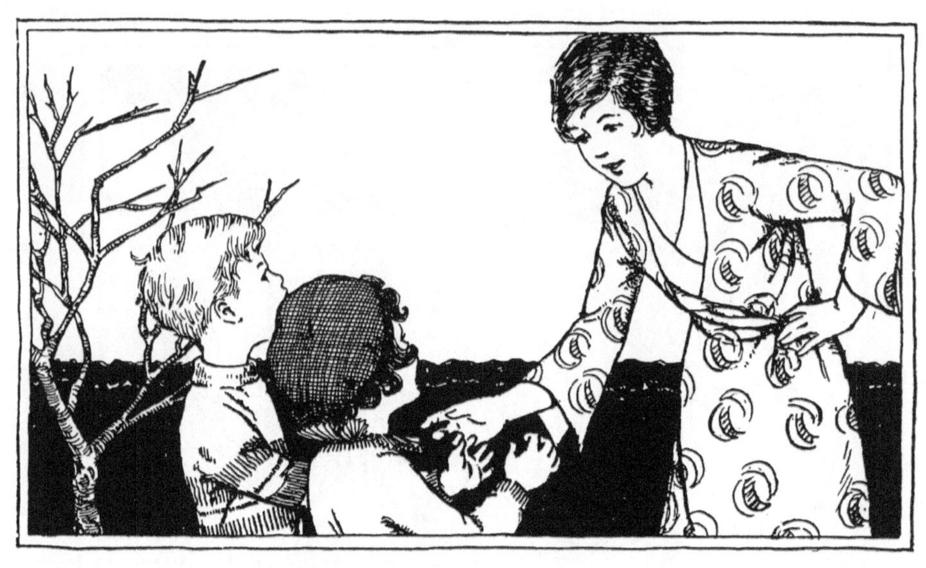

THE SCHOOL GARDEN

Ted and Ann went to school.

Their teacher was Miss Bell.

They told Miss Bell about hunting.

"We played a game," said Ann.

"The game was Hunting for Holes,"
said Ted.

Miss Bell smiled and said,
    "That was a very good game.
    Do you wish to play a new game?"

"What is the new game?" asked Ted.

Miss Bell said, "You may call it
    Hunting in the School Garden."

"May we hunt today?" asked Ann.

"Yes, you may," said their teacher.

"How shall we hunt?" asked Ted.

Then Miss Bell told them,
    "Hunt for plants and animals.
    You may find an animal that hops.
    You may find one that flies."

THE SLEEPY TOAD

A man was digging
   in the school garden.

"Why do you dig?" asked Ted.

"The ground is hard," said the man.
   "Most plants need soft ground."

The man dug up some more soil.
He dug up a toad, too!
The toad did not hop or move.
It did not open its eyes.

"What a quiet toad!" said Ted.

"Is the toad sleepy?" asked Ann.

"Yes," said the man, "put it in the sunshine and watch it.
Toads sleep in the winter while
they are cold.
They wake in the warm spring."

Ted put the toad in the sunshine.
He watched it open its eyes.
At last, it hopped.

Ted took the toad in his hands.
He showed it to Miss Bell.

"Shall we give it food?" asked Ann.

"No," said Miss Bell, "please put it
near the pond in the park.
It will be glad to find water."

"Do toads go to ponds?" asked Ted.
    "Do they go to water like frogs?"

Miss Bell said, "Toads live on land,
    and they live in water, too.
    In spring, they go to water.
    They sit in the water and sing.
    Toads lay their eggs in water.
    Baby tadpoles hatch from the eggs.
    Tadpoles grow to be toads."

Ann asked, "May we keep tadpoles
    in school when they hatch?"

"Yes," said Miss Bell, "if you
    will take good care of them."

So they took the toad to the pond.

Eleanor Osborn Eadie

LITTLE RED TRUMPETS

A plant grew in the school garden.

It was about six years old.

Its roots were in the ground.

Its stems climbed up a tree.

It had no leaves in winter.

The plant had new leaves in spring.
It had flowers in spring, too.
The flowers were red and yellow.
They were long like little trumpets.

Ted asked Miss Bell about the flowers
in the school garden.
He said, "Have they any nectar?"

She said, "Yes, they have nectar, and
it is like sweet water."

"The flowers are long," said Ted.
"What can get the nectar?"

Miss Bell smiled and said,
"Watch the flowers someday, and
perhaps you will see!"

HUMMINGBIRDS

Two birds came to the red flowers.

They were very, very little, but they had long bills.

The birds put their long bills into the flowers to take nectar.

Ted and Ann watched the two birds.
They were quiet while they watched.
Ted and Ann could hear the
    humming sound of the wings.

One bird was Father Hummingbird,
    and one was Mother Hummingbird.
Father Hummingbird had a green
    back and a red throat.

Mother Hummingbird had a green
    back and a white throat.
Ted and Ann ran to tell Miss Bell.
Ann said, "We saw some little birds
    with humming wings.
    They put their long bills
    into the red trumpets for nectar!"

FORGET-ME-NOT

One day, Miss Bell asked,
 "Who hunted in the garden today?"

"Ann and I hunted today," said Ted,
 "and we found a pretty plant."

"It had pink buds," said Ann,
 "and its flowers were blue."

Miss Bell said, "Please cut a stem
   for each boy and girl."

Ted cut the stems, and then each boy
   and girl took one.

Miss Bell said, "There are no roots on
   the stems Ted cut for you.
But there are leaves and flowers.
Watch the stems each day."

Miss Bell filled a glass with water.
Then she said, "Each boy and girl may
   put a stem into this glass."

The boys and girls put the stems into
   the glass and watched them.

One day Ann said, "See the stems in
   the glass of water!
There are white roots on them!"

"The stems are plants now with
roots," said Ted.

The boys and girls took the stems
into the school garden.
They put the stems into wet ground
and put soil on the new roots.

So each boy and girl had a plant.
Its name was forget-me-not.

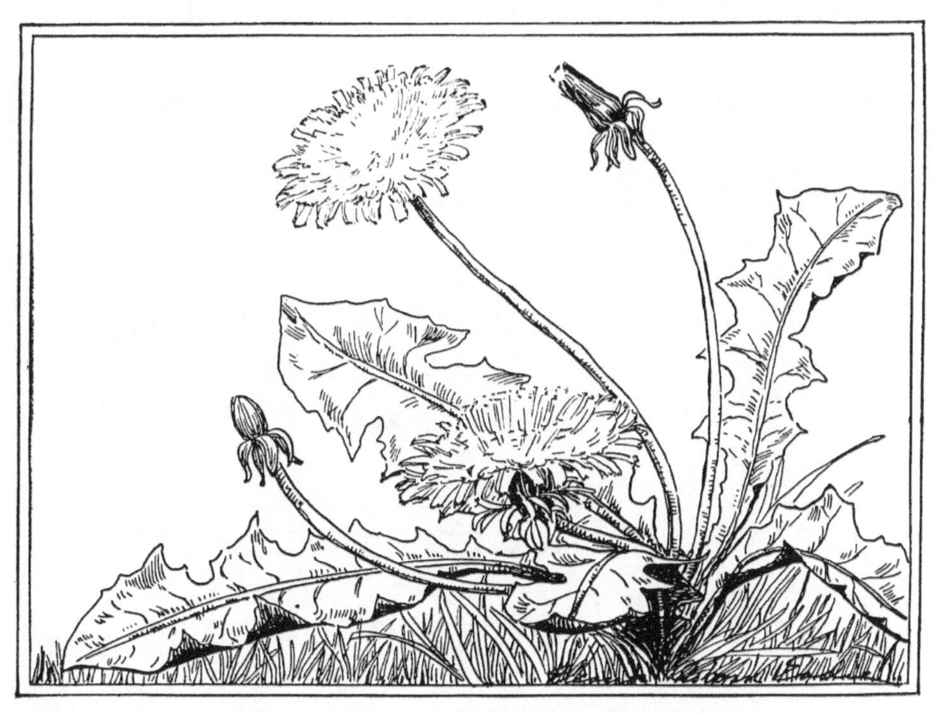

A WEED

A plant grew in the school garden.

Its name was dandelion.

Its leaves were near the ground.

The dandelion flowers were yellow.

They grew on the tops of long stems.

One day the boys and girls went into
	the school garden.
They saw the dandelion plant.

A girl said, "Dandelions are weeds.
	We do not let them grow at home."

A boy said, "They are good to eat.
	I dig dandelions each spring.
	Mother cooks the young plants."

Ted asked, "What is a weed?"

Miss Bell said, "A weed is a plant that
	people do not like to have.
	Dandelions are often weeds.
	They are weeds when they grow
	where people wish other plants."

Seeds grew on the flower stems.

Then the long dandelion stems had
  pretty white heads.

The boys and girls liked to play with
  the white seed heads.

They watched the little seeds.

The seeds went away with the wind.

THE RED LILY

Uncle Jim gave Ted a bulb, and he
gave Ann some seeds.
Uncle Jim said, "I found the bulb,
and I found the seeds.
They grew on a lily plant."

Ted showed his bulb to Miss Bell.

She said, "You may put it in the
  school garden."

So Ted dug a hole in the ground and
  put his bulb into it.
Then he put some soil on the bulb.

The bulb rested in the ground.
It rested all the cold winter days.

The ground was warm in spring.

So the bulb was warm then, too.

The warm bulb grew in the sunshine.

A stem grew up from the bulb.

There were long leaves on the stem.

Ted hunted for his plant in spring.

He found it in the sunshine.

He told Miss Bell about it.

"The lily has a stem with leaves, but it
has no flowers," he said.

Miss Bell said, "You may hunt in the
school garden this summer.
You and Ann may watch the lily.
Perhaps you will find a flower if
you hunt for it in summer."

Ted's lily had flowers in summer.

Ted went to the garden to see them.

Ann went with him.

The flowers were red and brown.

There was brown pollen in them.

Some little bees came for pollen.

Ted and Ann watched the bees.

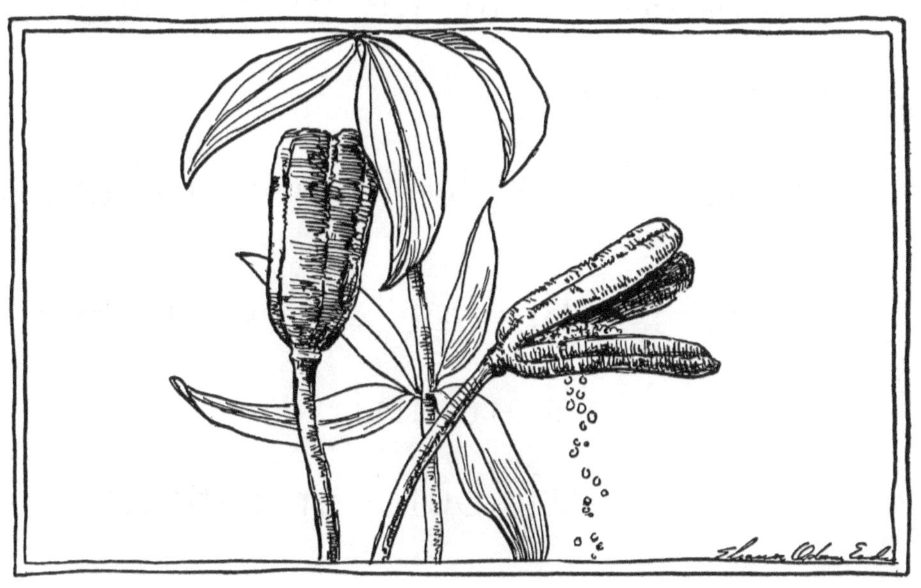

Ann told Miss Bell about the seeds
  that Uncle Jim gave her.
Miss Bell said,
  "You may plant them
  in the school garden."

So Ann put the seeds in the garden.
The lily seeds rested all winter.

Ann hunted for her lily plants when
summer came.
Then she told Uncle Jim about them.

"Ted's lily is a big one," she said, "but
my lily plants are little.
They have little bulbs and stems."

He said, "Your plants are too young
to have flowers this year."

"When will they be old enough to
have flowers?" asked Ann.

"When they are four years old," said
her uncle.
"Then they will have big bulbs like
the bulb I gave to Ted."

WHAT IS IT?

Toads go to it in spring.
Mother Toad puts her eggs in it.
The baby toads live in it.
What is it?

It is like sweet water.
Bumblebees find it in flowers.
Hummingbirds drink it.
What is it?

It has a bulb in the ground.
It has long green leaves.
It has red and brown flowers.
What is it?

WORD GAME

How will you use each word?

pink   green   blue   throat

nectar   weeds   winter   wind

The forget-me-not flowers are __.

The forget-me-not buds are __.

The dandelion seeds went away with
the __.

Father Hummingbird had a red __.

His back was __.

Hummingbirds put their long bills
into long flowers for __.

The toad was sleepy in __.

People do not like some plants, and
they call them __.

IF I FIND A FLOWER

If I find a flower,
   I'll watch to see
If a hummingbird comes
   And a bumblebee!

There is nectar sweet
   In a flower cup.
I'll watch to see
   If they drink it up!

If you find a flower,
   Will you watch to see
If a hummingbird comes
   And a bumblebee?

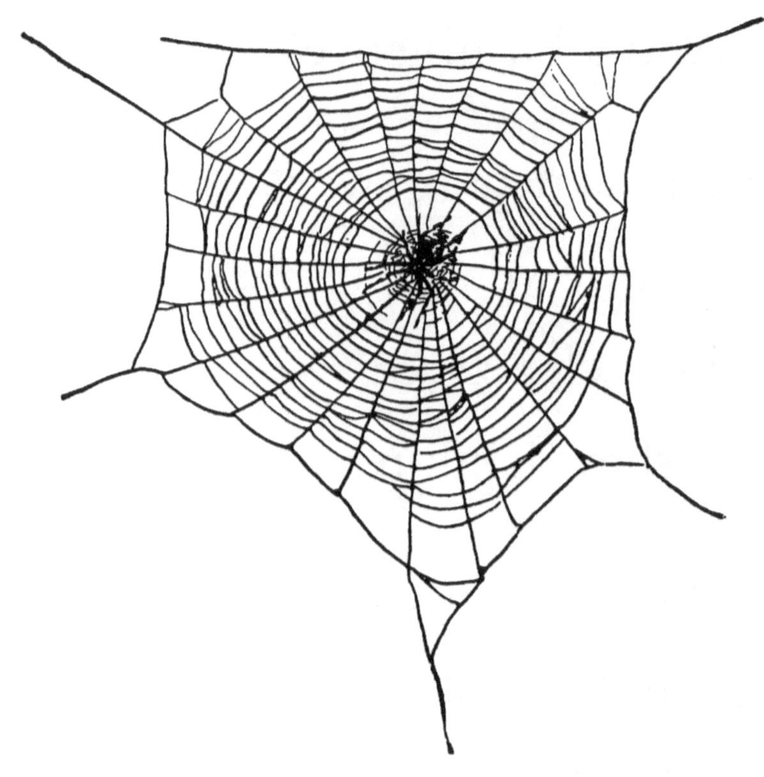

PART THREE
Hunting in the Park

THE PARK

A man took good care of the park.

His name was Mr. Long.

He told Ted and Ann about plants.

He told them about animals, too.

Mr. Long was their kind friend.

"The biggest plants in the park
  are the trees," said Mr. Long.

"May we help you take care
  of the trees?" asked Ted.

"You may help me when I cut off
  old dry branches," said Mr. Long.

"Some of the animals in the park
have fur," said Mr. Long.

"Squirrels have fur," said Ann.
"We will help take care of them."

So Ted and Ann gave peanuts
to the squirrels in the park.

"Some of the animals in the park
have feathers," said Mr. Long.

"Birds have feathers," said Ted.
"Uncle Jim gave us a box for the
birds.
Will you put it up on a tree?"

"Yes," said Mr. Long, "I will."

Father and Mother Bluebird came
and made a nest in the box.
They made it with brown dry grass.

Mother Bluebird liked to hear Father
Bluebird sing his songs.

There were four pretty blue eggs in
the bluebird nest.
Mother Bluebird kept them warm.

When the four young birds hatched,
they were hungry.
They all opened their mouths.

So their father and mother hunted.
The old birds found food for the
hungry young bluebirds.

One day Ted and Ann told Mr. Long
about their hunting games.

"We played one game," said Ann.
"Its name was Hunting for Holes."

"The other game we played,"
said Ted, "was Hunting
in the School Garden."

Mr. Long smiled and asked them, "Do
you wish to play a new game?
You may call it
Hunting in the Park."

Ted said, "That is a good game, too!"

"We will hunt to-day," said Ann.
So Ted and Ann went hunting.

TOADS AND TADPOLES

One spring day Ted and Ann hunted
near the pond in the park.

They could hear a song there.

They saw a toad in the pond.

He was fat Father Toad.

Father Toad had a very good song.
It had a high sound
   like a high sweet whistle.
It had a soft low sound, too.
Father Toad did not open his mouth
   to sing high and low sounds.
But his throat was round
   like a little balloon.

Mother Toad was in the pond, too,
   but she had no song to sing.
She did not make her throat round
   like a little balloon.
She liked sweet songs in spring.
So she came near while Father Toad
   made high sounds and low sounds.

Mother Toad laid eggs in the pond.

She did not sit on her eggs.

Her body was cold, and so
   she could not keep her eggs warm.

She went away from them.

The eggs were warm without her.

The sunshine made them warm.

Baby toads were in the eggs.

We call baby toads tadpoles.

They hatched in the warm sunshine.

They were not like grown toads.

The tadpoles had no legs at all, but
they had long tails.

They could swim with their tails.

The young tadpoles were hungry.
Father and Mother Toad did not
    hunt for their tadpoles.
The tadpoles hunted their own food.
They changed shape as they grew.
Their mouths were not so little, and
    their tails were not so big.

The tadpoles all had legs when they
grew old enough.
First each tadpole had two legs.
Then each of them had three legs.
After a while, each one had four legs
and no tail.

So the tadpoles changed to toads.
They were very little toads.
The body of each young toad was
about half an inch long.

One day some rain wet the ground.
The little toads liked the rain.
They came out of the water and
hopped on the ground.
After that, they hunted on land.

Ted and Ann came out in the rain.

They came to the park to play.

They hunted near the pond and
  found the young toads.

They watched the little toads while
  they hopped on the ground.

Then Ted and Ann hopped, too!

PUSSY WILLOWS

Ted and Ann hunted in the park and
found willows near the pond.
The willows had many branches.
Willow flowers grew on the branches.
But some were not like the others.

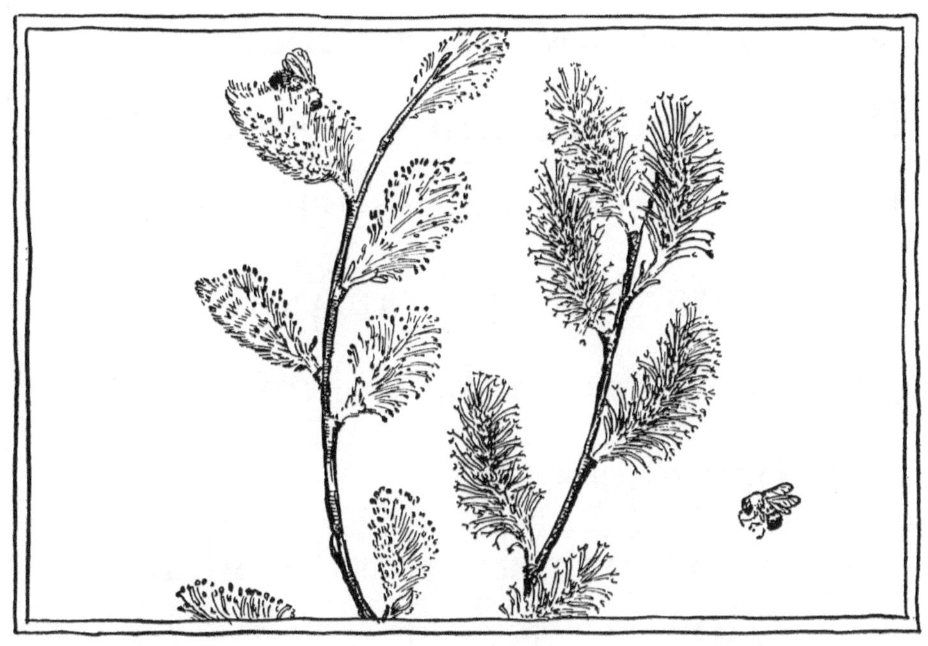

One willow had flowers with nectar
and pollen but no seeds.

One willow had flowers with nectar
and seeds but no pollen.

The baby seeds in the flowers could
not live without pollen.

How did the seeds get some pollen?

Little bees took the pollen.

The bees did not know about seeds.

They did not know that the seeds
could not live without pollen.

The bees went to the willows for food
for baby bees.

They went for nectar and pollen.

Some pollen fell on them like dust.

So they took it on their hairs to the
flowers without pollen.

Some fell from the hairs like dust
when they went there for nectar.

That is how the young willow seeds
could have pollen and live.

The willows gave the bees food, and
the bees helped the willows.

One day Mr. Long told Ted and Ann
about willow flowers and bees.

He said, "Bumblebees and honey bees
and other bees come to willows.
They come for nectar and pollen.
Honey bees make very good honey
from nectar in willow flowers."

Ted and Ann liked honey to eat.
They often came to the willows to
watch the honey bees.

"The flowers are pretty," said Ann.
"Some parts of them are yellow.
Some parts are gray and as soft as
the fur a pussy has."

Ted said, "Perhaps that is why people
call them pussy willows."

Ann asked, "Are you glad bees find
pollen on this bush and take it to
that other willow?
So that willow can have seeds!"

"Yes," said Ted, "I should say I am!"

ROBINS

Father Robin lived in the park and so
did Mother Robin.

Robin liked to sing in spring.

Father Robin liked to hear him sing.

His spring song had a happy sound.

Father Robin had a black head with a
little white near his eyes.

His throat was white and black, and
his bill was yellow.

He had a gray back and a red front.

Mother Robin looked very much like
Father Robin.

Mother Robin hunted in a tree and
    found a good branch.
Then she made a nest on the branch.
She made it with mud and old grass.
She could use mud while it was wet.
So she made the mud nest a good
    shape to sit in.
She put in some dry brown grass.
Then it was a soft nest for eggs.

Mother Robin laid one egg each day
    for four days.
So she had four eggs in her nest.
She sat on them and kept them warm.

Father Robin hunted for food and
    gave Mother Robin some of it.

Ted and Ann found the nest and
asked Mr. Long about it.

Mr. Long held Ann up to the nest so
she could see the eggs.
"What pretty blue eggs!" said Ann.

Then Mr. Long held Ted up to see.
"What pretty green eggs!" Ted said.

Ann and Ted and Mr. Long laughed.
"Are the eggs blue?" asked Ted.
"Are they green?" asked Ann.

"It is hard to tell," said Mr. Long,
"but most people call them blue."

Ted and Ann often came to the park
to see Mother and Father Robin.
They were quiet when they came and
did not scare the birds.
One day they saw four young robins
that could hop on the ground.
They were too young to fly.

A BROWN COCOON

Ted and Ann hunted in the park and found a brown cocoon.

The brown cocoon was on a branch.

It had been there all winter.

Ted and Ann found it one spring day.

A caterpillar made the cocoon.

It made the cocoon with silk.

The caterpillar had some glands in its
body.

The silk came from the glands.

The silk came out of a hole near the
mouth of the caterpillar.

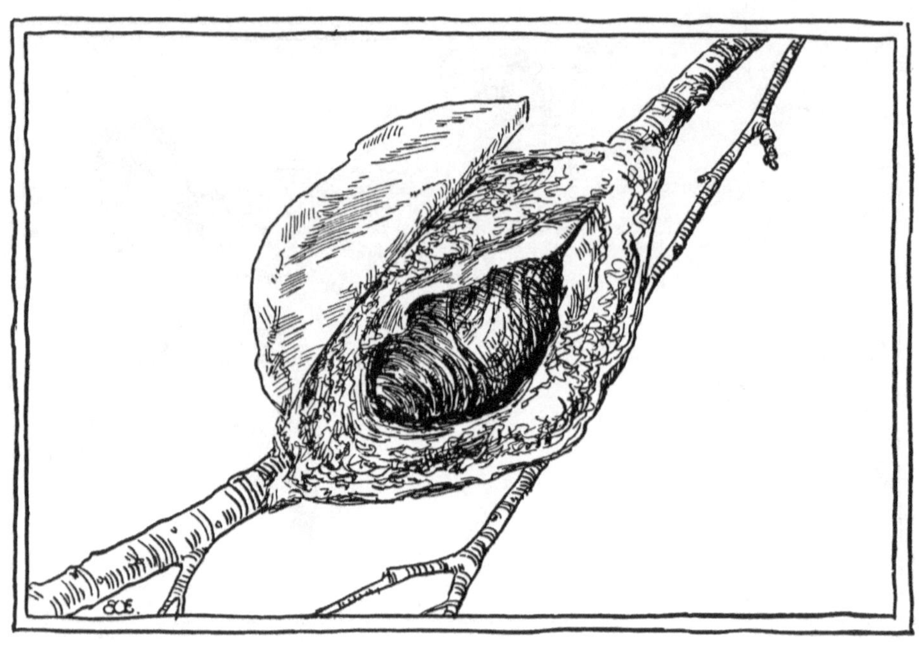

The caterpillar made the cocoon all
around its body.

Then the caterpillar changed into a
brown pupa.

The pupa had no mouth or legs.

The pupa could not eat or creep.

It rested in the cocoon all winter.

Ted and Ann found the cocoon, and
Mr. Long told them about it.

"A big green caterpillar made that
cocoon," he said.
"It had sharp spines on its body.
They were red, blue, and yellow."

"It had pretty colors!" said Ann.

"Where did it come from?" said Ted.

"A moth laid an egg," said Mr. Long,
"with a baby caterpillar in it.
The caterpillar hatched and grew.
Then it made a silk cocoon and
changed into a brown pupa.
Some day it will be a pretty moth."

"May we have the cocoon?"
    asked Ted.

Mr. Long gave them the cocoon, and
    they took it to Miss Bell.

She showed it to the girls and boys.

"What is in it?" asked a boy.

"A pupa is in it," said Miss Bell.
"A moth laid an egg.
A caterpillar hatched from the egg.
It ate and grew and made a cocoon.
Then it changed to a pupa."

"What will the pupa change to?"
    asked one of the girls.
"Wait and see!" said Miss Bell.

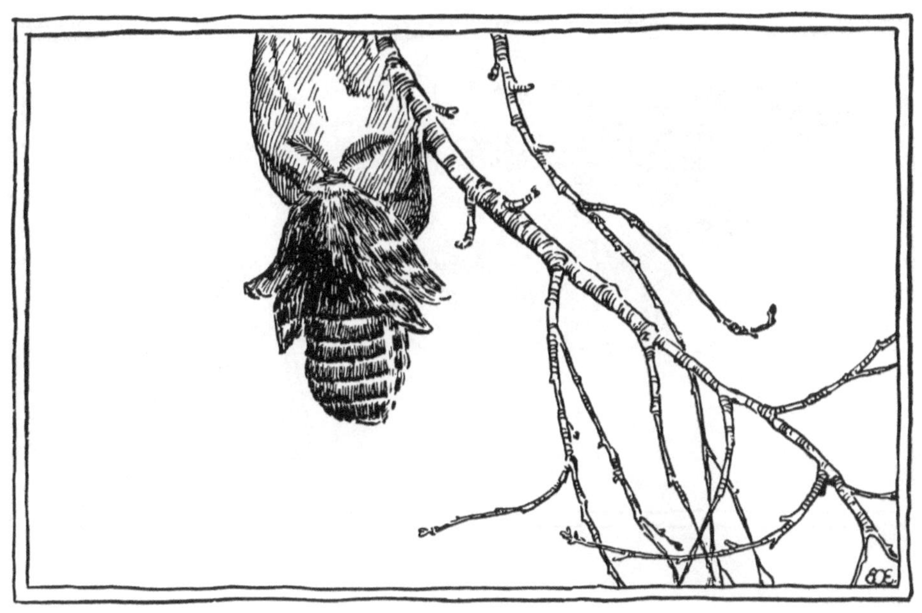

One day Miss Bell said,
   "I hear a sound in the cocoon."

The boys and girls all watched it.

A moth came out of the cocoon.
It had two feelers on its head.
The feelers looked like feathers.

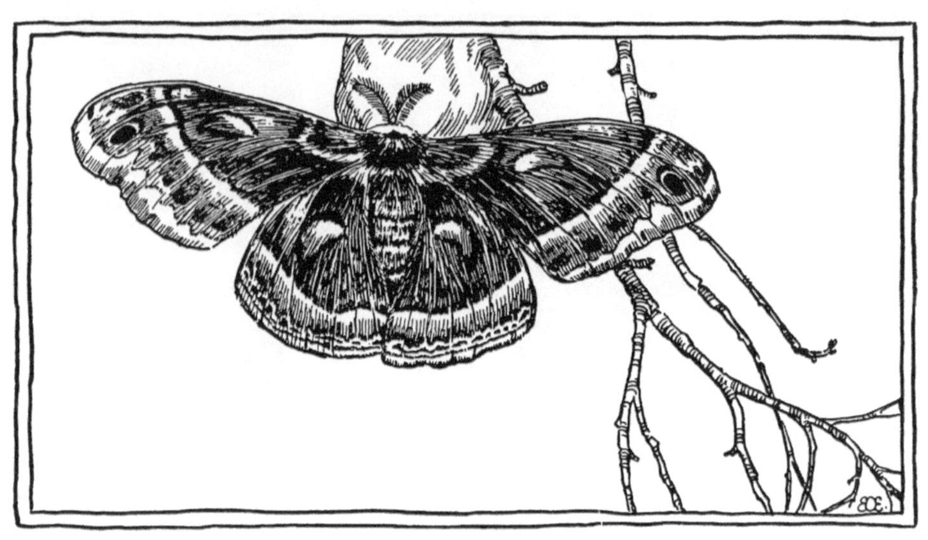

The moth had four wings.

At first, the wings were little.

The boys and girls
    watched them grow.

The wings were light and dark brown
    with red and white on them.

There were two black spots with
    some pretty blue on them.

Miss Bell said,
    "If we keep the moth in school,
    it will fly to the window
    and break its wings."

"Will it fly today?" asked Ann.

"No," said Miss Bell, "it will wait and
    fly in the night."

"I will take it outdoors," said Ted,
    "and put it on a tree."

Then Ted put the moth on a branch.
It rested there all that day.
The moth woke when night came.
It liked the dark night.
So the moth flew away in the dark.

ACORNS

An old oak tree lived in the park.

Many acorns grew on the oak tree.

The acorns were seeds of the oak.

They had hard brown shells.

A baby oak tree was in each shell.

Some squirrels hunted for acorns.

They liked acorns to eat.

They put acorns in holes in trees.

They put acorns in the ground, too.

They dug up some when winter came.

But some they left in the ground and
did not find all winter.

The ground was warm in spring, and
    rain wet the acorn shells.

In spring the baby oak trees grew too
    big for their shells.
The hard brown acorn shells broke,
    and the little trees sprouted.

Ted and Ann hunted in the park and
    found many young oaks.
Then they went to tell Mr. Long.

"Mr. Long, please come to see how
    the acorns grew!" said Ann.

Mr. Long went with Ted and Ann.
He looked at the young trees.
He said, "The trees are too thick."

Mr. Long said, "You may have all the young oaks you will dig."

Ted and Ann dug some little trees and put them in a box.

"Mr. Long, we thank you for so many young oak trees," they said.

Ted and Ann showed their young
oaks to Uncle Jim.

"Wet the roots," said Uncle Jim.
"We will plant them Saturday."

On Saturday their uncle said,
"Take your trees to my car, and we
will go to the old farm."

So they all went to the farm where
Uncle Jim had lived when he was a
boy as young as Ted.

Uncle Jim showed Ted and Ann
where to plant their trees.
There was a good place for them to
grow, near a wall.

Ted and Ann were very happy about
their little oak trees.

"When they grow old enough, they
will have acorns," said Ann.

"Perhaps some squirrels will hunt and
find the acorns," said Ted.

"Yes," said Ann, "and perhaps they
will put some in the wall and eat
them in winter."

"Perhaps they will put some in the
ground, too!" said Ted.
"Some acorns may grow, and then
there will be more oak trees on the
farm."

"I hope we may see these trees when
they have acorns," said Ann.
"We shall be grown," said Ted, "when
these oaks have acorns.
Perhaps we shall be as old as
Uncle and Mother and Father!"

SWANS

Two white swans lived in the park.
They were Father and Mother Swan.
Their bodies were a little like boats,
and their feet were a little like
paddles.

Ted and Ann often came to see the swans swim in the pond.

"They move in the water like boats," said Ted, "with feet for paddles."

"What long necks they have and how they bend them!" said Ann.

One day there were six gray swans
near the two white swans.

"Mr. Long," said Ann,
"will you please tell us about
the six gray swans?"

Mr. Long told them,
"Mother Swan laid some eggs.
These birds came from her eggs."

"Will their gray feathers fall out and
new feathers grow?" said Ann.

"Yes," said Mr. Long, "and then the six
young swans will be white like their
father and mother."

A WATER LILY

When warm summer came, Ted and
Ann hunted for summer flowers.
One day they found a water lily in
the pond in the park.
It was white and green and yellow.

The outside of the lily was green.

The middle parts were yellow.

All the other parts were white.

Many bees came to get lily pollen.

They took some to their young bees.

Flies often came to eat pollen for
their own food.

They did not take it to young flies.

One day Mr. Long told Ted and Ann
about the bees and flies.

"Each bee has four wings," he said,
"and each fly has two wings."

So Ted and Ann looked at the wings
of the bees and the flies.

AN ANIMAL WITH
EIGHT LEGS

Ted and Ann went to see Mr. Long.

He said, "Today I saw an animal.
What do you think it was?"

So they asked about the animal.

"It has no fur," said Mr. Long.

"Then it was not a mole," said Ann, "or a squirrel or a woodchuck."

"It had no feathers," said Mr. Long.

"Then it was not a robin," said Ted, "or a bluebird or a woodpecker or a hummingbird or a swallow or any other kind of bird."

"Did it have six legs?" asked Ann.

"It had more than six," he said.

"Then it was not an ant," said Ann, "or any other grown insect. All grown insects have six legs."

"It made silk," said Mr. Long.

"Caterpillars make silk," said Ted.

"The animal I saw," said Mr. Long, "was not a caterpillar."

"How many legs did the animal have?" asked Ann.

"It had eight legs," said Mr. Long.

"Will you please tell us what animal has eight legs?" asked Ann.

Mr. Long smiled and said, "No, I will not tell you what it is."

So they hunted in the park to find an animal that had eight legs!

Ted and Ann found a little animal
  without feathers or fur.

It was on a pretty silk web.

Its back was brown and yellow.

It had eight eyes and eight legs.

The animal on the silk web was a
  spider.

The spider had glands in her body.
Some of them were silk glands.

Silk came out of the silk glands when
  the spider needed it.
The silk was like very fine thread.

The spider made a web with silk.
The web was her home in summer.
It was a good home for her.

Some flies came to her web, and they
  could not get away.
They could not walk on the silk.

The spider could walk on her web.
She took the flies and ate them.
The flies were good food for her.

The spider laid eggs in the fall.

She did not lay them in her web.

She put some soft white silk around
her eggs for a nest.

This nest was round like a ball.

Baby spiders hatched in the nest.

Some day they would make webs,
too.

CAN YOU TELL?

Did Mother Toad warm her eggs or
did the sun keep them warm?

Do ants and bees have six legs or do
they have eight legs?

Do acorns grow on oak trees or do
they grow on willow trees?

Do old swans have gray feathers and
are young swans white?

Was the cocoon made by a moth
or was it made by a caterpillar
or was it made by a pupa?

WHAT WAS IT?

It had eight legs.
It made a silk web.
It liked to eat flies.
What was it?

It grew in a pond.
It was white and green and yellow.
Bees came to it for pollen.
What was it?

It rested all day.
It woke when night came.
It flew away in the dark.
What was it?

THE PARK IS A HAPPY PLACE TO BE

The park is a happy place to be,
There are so many things to see!

I like the pond in early spring,
For then the frogs begin to sing.

In summer time I like the breeze
And humming sounds of little bees.

In fall the squirrels hunt and play
And hide their many nuts away.

When winter comes, the park is
    white,
And sunshine seems so very bright!

PART FOUR
Hunting in the Zoo

FATHER'S GAME

Ted and Ann often talked with their
father and mother about hunting.
They told them about all the games
they liked to play with Uncle Jim
and Miss Bell and Mr. Long.

One day their father said to them,
	"You are very good hunters.
	You find bees and birds and toads
	and little animals with fur.
	You are quiet and watch to see how
	they look and what they do.

"You help take care of plants and
	watch to see their flowers grow.
	You do not often break the stems,
	but leave the flowers for other boys
	and girls to see and like."

Then Father smiled and asked them,
	"Will you come to hunt with me?
	I know a good hunting game.
	I call it Hunting in the Zoo."

THE ZOO

Part of the zoo was like a park.

There were many ponds in the park.

Big pink birds waded in one pond.

There were trees in the zoo and some
deer ran near the trees.

There were big stones in the zoo and
some bears climbed the stones.

"May we see the bears?" asked Ted.

"May we see the deer?" asked Ann.

Father smiled and looked at Ted.
"Ann may choose first," said Ted.

So they all went to watch the deer.

DEER WITH WHITE TAILS

"See their white tails!" said Ann.

"Are all deer like these?" asked Ted.

"No," said their father,
  "there are different kinds.
  Some do not have white tails."

Father White tails have horns.
Their horns are not like the horns
    that a cow has.

A deer has horns with branches.
A cow has horns without branches.

The horns of white-tail deer fall off
    their heads each year.
Then new horns grow on their heads.

If people cut the horns off a cow, new
    horns do not grow.

Ted and Ann looked at the horns on
    the heads of the father deer.
They asked Father about the horns
    that deer and cows have.

"See that little deer!" said Ann.

"It has white spots," said Ted.

"It is a baby deer," said Father.
"Its first hair will fall out.
New brown hair will grow and then
the young deer will have no spots."

"Do baby cows have spots?" said Ted.

"They have no spots like these, but their first hair falls out and new hair grows," said Father.

"Do the old deer and the old cows have new hair, too?" asked Ted.

"Yes," said Father, "old cows and old deer have new hair each year."

Then Ted said, "Look at their feet! Deer have hoofs and so do cows."

"There are some other kinds of deer in this zoo," said Father.

So they went to see the other deer.

BEARS

Father went with Ted and Ann to see
all the bears in the zoo.

The bears lived in outdoor cages.
The cages were kept clean for them.
The cages were in the sunshine.

There were stones in the cages big
enough for bears to climb.

There were holes near the stones big
enough for bears to sleep in.
The holes were clean and dry.

The bears played in the sunshine and
slept in the dark holes.

A brown bear was in one cage.

She could walk on her two hind feet.

The brown bear was very tame and
she liked to see people.

Ted and Ann laughed to see her walk
on her two hind feet.

There were six bears in one cage.

Their name was Black Bear.

Their fur was black and brown.

They could walk on all four feet.

They could walk on their hind feet.

There were old trees in their cage.

The black bears played and climbed.

Father said, "Once, I saw a bear climb
an old tree on the farm.
The tree had a big hole in it.
The hole was filled with honey.
Some bees had put it there.
The bear put his paws in the hole
and took out some of the honey.
He liked to eat sweet food."

"Did the bees sting him?" asked Ted.
"Did they scare the bear away?"

"The bees buzzed," said Father.
"Their buzzing was a cross sound.
But they could not hurt the bear.
His fur was too thick for them.
The bees could not scare the bear."

There were white bears in the zoo.

They had a good pond in their cage
and there was ice in it.

The bears liked to swim in the pond
and put their paws on the ice.

The zoo would be too warm for them
without the ice.

RACCOONS

One day Father and Ted and Ann went
to the zoo to hunt for raccoons.

They found two raccoons in a tree.

The raccoons were quiet in the tree.

They looked very sleepy.

After a while one of the raccoons
climbed down a tree and Ted and
Ann could see her face.

Part of her face was black and her
eyes were in the black part.
The fur on other parts of her body
had gray and brown and black and
yellow hairs in it.

"It is hard to tell," said Ann, "what
color a raccoon is!"

The raccoon did not walk on her toes
as a cat walks.
She put her feet flat on the ground
like a bear when it walks.

When the raccoons were hungry, they
   put their food in water.
Then they took it out and ate it.

"I wish we had a raccoon!" said Ted.

Father smiled and told him,
   "Raccoons are often good pets."

AN ANIMAL WITH SPINES

A boy came to the porcupine cage.

He opened the cage and went in.

The boy took a box into the cage.

It was large enough for a porcupine.

The boy was Robert Brown.

Robert moved slowly in the cage.
He did not scare the porcupines.

"Spiny, Spiny, come to me," he said,
"and I will take you home."

Spiny had a fat body and short legs
but he went as fast as he could.

Spiny made a soft happy sound.

"You are glad I came!" said Robert.
Robert rubbed his pet slowly.
He rubbed Spiny from head to tail.
He did not rub from tail to head.

Robert opened his box and said,
   "Are you hungry, Spiny?
   There is good food in the box."

Spiny climbed into the box and ate
   some of the food.

Robert closed the box and took it out
   of the porcupine cage.

He saw Ted and Ann and smiled.

"Would you like to see my pet?
It is a porcupine," said Robert.

"Yes, please, we should!" said Ted.

Ted and Ann looked at Spiny.
They saw his black and gray hairs.
Many of the hairs had white ends.

The porcupine had long sharp spines on his head and back and tail.

"Did your porcupine ever hurt you with his spines?" asked Ann.

"He would not hurt me," said Robert. "He would not hurt his friends."

"Would he hurt a dog?" asked Ted.

"He hurt a dog once," said Robert.
"The dog ran after him.
Spiny hit the dog with his tail.
Then the dog had spines in his
nose and they hurt.
I asked a man to take them out.
That dog did not
chase Spiny again!"

"You were kind to show us Spiny
and tell us about him," said Ted.

Then they all went home.

THE BIGGEST ANIMAL
IN THE ZOO

"An elephant is the biggest animal in the zoo," said Ted one day.

"I wish we could see one," said Ann.

So they went to the zoo with Father. They saw an elephant.

The elephant had a big heavy head.
Her head was too big and heavy for a
   long neck to hold up.
The elephant had a short neck.
She could not put her mouth down
   to the ground to eat.
She could not eat as a cow can.

So how could she get food to eat?

The elephant had a long nose.
Her nose was so long she could put
   the end of it down to the ground.
She could hold food with her nose
   and put it into her mouth.
So that is the way she ate!

Ted watched the elephant and said,
"An elephant eats with her nose.
Can she drink with her nose, too?"

"Watch her drink," said Father.

She put the end of her long nose into
water and took some water up into
the two holes in her nose.
Then she put the end of her nose
into her mouth and the water went
down her throat.

"How does she breathe?" asked Ann.

"As you do," said her father.
"She takes air into two holes in her
nose when she breathes."

"The long nose of an elephant has a
different name.

We call it a trunk," said Father.

"Her two biggest teeth are not like
the teeth most animals have.
We call these big teeth tusks."

"Shall we play a game," said Ted,
    "and tell how the elephant is
    different?"

"She has no horns on her head," said
    Ann, "so she is different from the
    cows at the farm."

"Her hair is not fur," said Ted,
    "so she is different from a mole."

"Her tail is not so big as her nose,"
    said Ann, "so she is different from a
    squirrel or a cat."

Father laughed and said,
    "She has five hoofs on each foot.
    So she is different from a deer."

SOME ZOO BIRDS

One day Ted and Ann went to the zoo
with their father to see the birds.

Many birds were in a big cage.

They flew about in the cage or sat in
the branches of a tree.

There were swans in the zoo pond.
Some were white and some were black.

"Are the black swans the young of the
white swans?" asked Ted.

"Will their new feathers be white like
the others?" asked Ann.

"No, the black swans are old birds,"
said Father, "and their new feathers
will be black, too."

There were geese in the zoo pond.
The geese were much like swans but
they were not so big and their necks
were not so long.
Their flat feet were like paddles.

There were ducks in the zoo pond.
The ducks were much like geese but
they were not so big and their
necks were not so long.
Their flat feet were like paddles.

There were many kinds of ducks with
feathers of different colors.

Some of the birds in the zoo pond
did not swim with paddle feet.
They waded with very long legs.

There were different kinds of birds
that waded in the water.
Their bodies had different shapes and
different colors.

Some of them were pink and white
with red and black feathers in their
pretty wings.

"See this pink bird!" said Ann.
"It likes to bend its long neck."

"It has a queer bill," said Ted.

A pink bird put its big bill into the
water and found food.

"It is a flamingo," said Father.
"One kind of flamingo is red."

"I wish I could see one," said Ann.
So they hunted for a red flamingo.

WHICH IS IT?

Which animal has horns?

    bear   deer   raccoon

Which bird swims in water?

    robin   bluebird   swan

Which animal has feathers?

    porcupine   bee   hummingbird

Which animal has four legs?

    elephant   spider   woodpecker

Which plant has blue flowers?

    dandelion   forget-me-not   water lily

Which animal has fur?

    frog   mole   ant

YES OR NO?

Do crickets have more wings than birds have?

Are insects and birds animals?

Do raccoons eat their food after they put it in water?

Do swans have feet shaped like the feet of robins?

Do insects have more feet than spiders have?

Do bank swallows dig holes with their feet?

Is the trunk of an elephant a long kind of mouth?

Word List

THE vocabulary of hunting comprises 485 different words. Derivatives are counted as separate words, except that such singular and plural forms as *bird* and *birds* or *sings* and *sing* are counted as one word.

Omitting six proper names, the number of words is 479. Of these 479 words, 415, or 87 percent, occur in the Gates list[1]; 407, or 85 percent, occur either in the first thousand words of the Gates list or in the first thousand words of the Thorndike list or of both; 333, or 70 percent, occur either in the first 500 words of the Gates list or of the Thorndike list or of both.

The rating of each word is here given in accordance with (1) the Gates list and (2) the Thorndike list[2]. The figure indicates the thousand; the letter a indicates the first half and the letter b indicates the second half of that thousand. Thus, 1a is used for a word that occurs in the first 500 words, 1b for a word of the second 500, 2a for a word of the third 500, and so on.

In the following list, the vocabulary of hunting is arranged by pages, each word being listed once and for the page on which it first appears.

[1]   A Reading Vocabulary for the Primary Grades by Arthur I. Gates.
[2]   The Teacher's Word Book by Edward L. Thorndike.

1
hunting 1b 1b
for 1a 1a
holes 1b 1b

2

3
Ted's — —
Ted — —
dug 1a 3b
a 1a 1a
he 1a 1a
the 1a 1a

with 1a 1a
spade — 3b

4
Ann — 7
came 1a 1a
to 1a 1a
see 1a 1a
my 1a 1a
said 1a 1a
it 1a 1a
is 1a 1a
big 1a 1a

5
good 1a 1a
game 1a 1a
uncle 1b 1b
Jim — 6
to-day 1a 1a
I 1a 1a
saw 1a 1a
some 1a 1a
little 1a 1a
we 1a 1a
will 1a 1a
hunt 1b 1b

and 1a 1a
find 1a 1a
be 1a 1b

6
ant 1b 4a
found 1a 1a
was 1a 1a
ran 1a 1b
into 1a 1a
out 1a 1a
of 1a 1a

7
each 1a 1a
had 1a 1a
six 1a 1a
legs 1a 1b
two 1a 1a
feelers — —
on 1a 1a
its 1a 1a
head 1a 1a
waved 2a 1b

8
mole — 5a
their 1a 1a
hands 1a 1a
were 1a 1a
blind — 1b
they 1a 1a
could 1a 1a
dig 1a 2b
without 1b 1a
seeing 1a 1a

9
fur 1b 2a
soft 1a 1a
warm 1a 1a
father 1a 1a
hunter 1b 2b
mother 1a 1a
too 1a 1a
hunted 1b 1b
in 1a 1a

10
nest 1a 1b
four 1a 1a

baby 1a 1b
took 1b 1a
care 1b 1a
she 1a 1a
do 1a 1a

11
swallow 2a 2a
birds 1a 1a
bank 1b 1a
bills 2a 1b
one 1a 1a
brown 1a 1b
white 1a 1a

12
made 1a 1a
laid 1a 1b
eggs 1a 1a
kept 2a 1b
grew 1b 1b
filled 1a 1a
shell 2a 2a
broke 2a 2b
hatched — 5a
flies 1a 3a
gave 1a 1a
not 1a 1a

13
day 1a 1a
his 1a 1a
pretty 1a 1a

14
squirrel 1a 3a
tree 1a 1a
gray 2a 1b

tail 1a 1b
liked 1a 1a
her 1a 1a

15
put 1a 1a
peanut 1b 7
near 1a 1a
sat 1a 1b
ground 1a 1a
very 1a 1a
quiet 2a 1b
down 1a 1a

16
helped 1a 1a
top 1a 1a
dry 1a 1b
leaves 1a 1a
lived 1a 1a
old 1a 1a
enough 1b 1a
climb 1a 2a
them 1a 1a

17

18
woodpecker 1b 6
no 1a 1a
this 1a 1a

19
perhaps 2a 1b
lives 1a 1a
shall 1a 1a
sit 1a 1a
bush 2a 2a

watch 1b 1a
flew 1b 2b
black 1a 1a
back 1a 1a
red 1a 1a
climbed 1a 2a
food 1a 1a

20
five 1a 1a
there 1a 1a
all 1a 1a
needed 2a 1a

21
so 1a 1a
young 2a 1a
hungry 1b 2a
or 1a 1a
fly 1a 1a
fed 1a 2b
ate 1a 2b
feathers 2a 2a
pick 1a 1b
tell 1a 1a

22
cricket — 4b
home 1a 1a
run 1a 1a
wings 1b 1b
but 1a 1a
happy 1b 1a
sound 1b 1a
like 1a 1a
cree-cree — —

23

while 1b 1a
watched 1b 1a
went 1a 1a
hear 1b 1a
make 1a 1a

24
winter 1a 1a
cold 1a 1a

25
spring 1b 1a
at 1a 1a

26
first 1a 1a
more 1b 1a
last 1b 1a
as 1a 1a
then 1a 1a
grown 1a 1a
sister 1a 1a
brother 1a 1a
glad 1a 1a

27
woodchuck — 9
him 1a 1a
grass 1a 1b

28
milk 1a 1a
play 1a 1a
drink 1a 1a
grow 1a 1a
when 1a 1a
played 1a 1a
sunshine 2a 2b
hind — 5a

use 1a 1a
paws 1b 5a
say 1a 1a
words 1b 1a
whistle — 2a
that 1a 1a
wav 1a 1a
talked 1b 1a

29
did 1b 1a
talk 1b 1a

30
often 1b 1a
eat 1a 1a
flowers 1a 2a
candy 1a 1b
held 2a 1b
laughed 1a 1a

31
bumblebee — —
hummed — 5b
humming — 5b
song 1a 1b

32
mouse 1a 2a
moved 2a 1a
bee 1a 1b
bread 1a 1a
honey 2a 2a
pollen — —
nectar — —
sweet 1b 1a
water 1a 1a
changed 2a 1a

yellow 1a 1b
dust 2a 1b

33
hairs 1a 1a
fat 1b 1b

34
sleep 1a 1a
rested 1a 1a
cocoons — 10
waked 2a 2a

35
buzzing 1b 3b
cross 1a 1a
buzzed 1b 3b
sting — 3a
you 1a 1a
if 1a 1a
go 1a 1a
take 1a 1a

36
may 1a 1a
are 1a 1a
rose 1b 1b

37
where 1a 1a
how 1a 1a

38

39
I'll 1a 2b
keep 1a 1a
still — 1a

40
school 1a 1a
garden 1a 1a

41

42
teacher 1a 2b
Miss 1a 1a
bell 1a 1b
told 1b 1b
about 1a 1a

43
smiled 1b 1b
new 1a 1a
what 1a
asked 1a 1a
call 1a 1a
yes 1a 1b
plants 1a 1a
animals 1b 1b
hops 1a 3a

44
sleepy — 3b
toad 1a 1a
man 10 2b
digging 1a 2b
why 1a 1a
hard 1b 1a
most 1b 1a
need 2a 1a

45
up 1a 1a
soil — 1b
move 2a 1a

open 1a 1a
eyes 1a 1a
wake 2a 2a
hopped 1a 3a

46
showed 1a 1a
please 1a 1a
pond 2a 2b
park 1b 2a

47
frogs 1b 3a
land 1b 1a
sing 1a 1a
tadpoles — 8
hatch — 5a
from 1a 1a

48

49
trumpets — 3a
years 1b 1a
roots 2a 2a
stems — 3a

50
long 1a 1a
any 1a 1a
can 1a 1a
get 1a 1a

51
humming- —
birds

52
green 1a 1a

throat — 2b

53
forget-me- —
not 1a 1a
who 1a 1a
pink 1b 2b
buds — 2b
blue 1a 1a

54
cut 1a 1a
boy 1a 1a
girl 1a 1a
are 1a 1a

55
glass 2a 1b

56
now 1a 1a
wet 1a 2a
name 1a 1a

57
weed — 2b
dandelion 1b 7

58
let 1a 1a
cooks 1b 1b
people 1a 1a
have 1a 1a
where 1a 1a
wish 1a 1a
other 1b 1a

59
seeds 1a 1b
away 1a 1a

wind 1a 1a

60
lily 1b 3a
bulb — 5b

61

62

63
summer 1a 1a
has 1a 1a

64

65

66
your 1a 1a

67

68

69
comes 1a 1a
cup 1a 1b

70

71

72
Mr. 1a 1b
kind 1b 1a
friend 1a 1a

73
biggest 1a 1a
help 1a 1a
me 1a 1a
off 1a 1a
branches 2a 1b

74

75

76
us 1a 1a
box 1a 1a

77
bluebird 1a 7
opened 1a 1a
mouths 1b 1b

78

79

80
high 1b 1a
low 1b 1a
round 1a 1a
balloon 1b 8

81
body 1b 1a

82
swim 1b 2a

83
own 1a 1a

9 781761 538384